# All You Need
# for a Snowman

*Illustrated by*

# BARBARA LAVALLEE

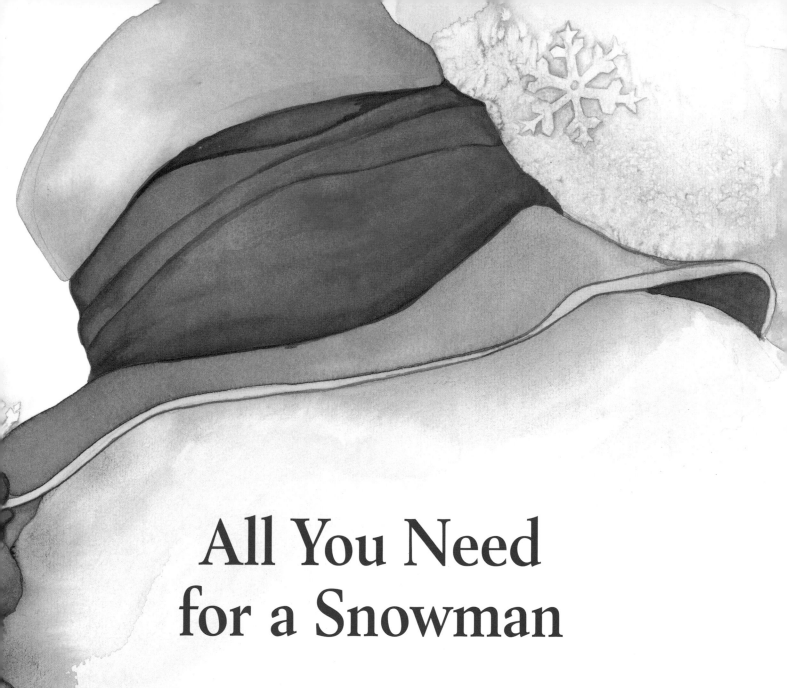

# All You Need
# for a Snowman

ALICE SCHERTLE

VOYAGER BOOKS • HARCOURT, INC.
Orlando  Austin  New York  San Diego  Toronto  London

For information about permission to reproduce selections from this
book, write to trade.permissions@hmhco.com or to Permissions,
Houghton Mifflin Harcourt Publishing Company, 3 Park Avenue,
19th Floor, New York, New York 10016.

www.hmhco.com

First Voyager Books edition 2007

*Voyager Books* is a trademark of Harcourt, Inc.,
registered in the United States of America and/or other jurisdictions.

The Library of Congress has cataloged the hardcover edition as follows:
Schertle, Alice.
All you need for a snowman/Alice Schertle; illustrated by Barbara Lavallee.
p.   cm.
Summary: Lists everything that one needs to build the perfect snowman,
from the very first snowflake that falls.
[1. Snowmen—Fiction.]   I. Lavallee, Barbara, ill.   II. Title.
PZ7.S3442Al   2002
[E]—dc21      2001004787
ISBN 978-0-15-200789-8
ISBN 978-0-15-206115-9 pb

SCP 15 14 13 12 11
4500735066

The illustrations in this book were done in watercolor and gouache on watercolor paper.
The display type and text type were set in Berling.
Color separations by Bright Arts Ltd., Hong Kong
Printed in China by RR Donnelley
Production supervision by Christine Witnik
Designed by Linda Lockowitz

To Spence and Dylan, pretty good snow men themselves
—A. S.

For Don Conrad, who knows all there is to know about snow
—B. L.

One small snowflake
fluttering down—

that's all you need
for a snowman.

EXCEPT

two more snowflakes...
three flakes...four...

five…six…seven thousand…
eight million more…

*Billions* of snowflakes
piled in a mound,
pat them
and pack them
and roll them
around

into one big ball.

And that's all.

One
big cold
well-rolled
snowflake ball—

that's all you need
for a snowman.

EXCEPT

for a middle-sized ball

and a small one.

On top of that
you need a hat.

A short flat hat or

a
tall
one.

Three hand-packed,
triple-stacked
balls of snow.

Hat on top,
where a hat should go—

that's all you need
for a snowman.

EXCEPT for

a couple of bottle caps,
round and flat—
stick them under
a snowman's hat.

SURPRISE!
Snowman's eyes!

That's all you need for
a snowman's face.

BUT

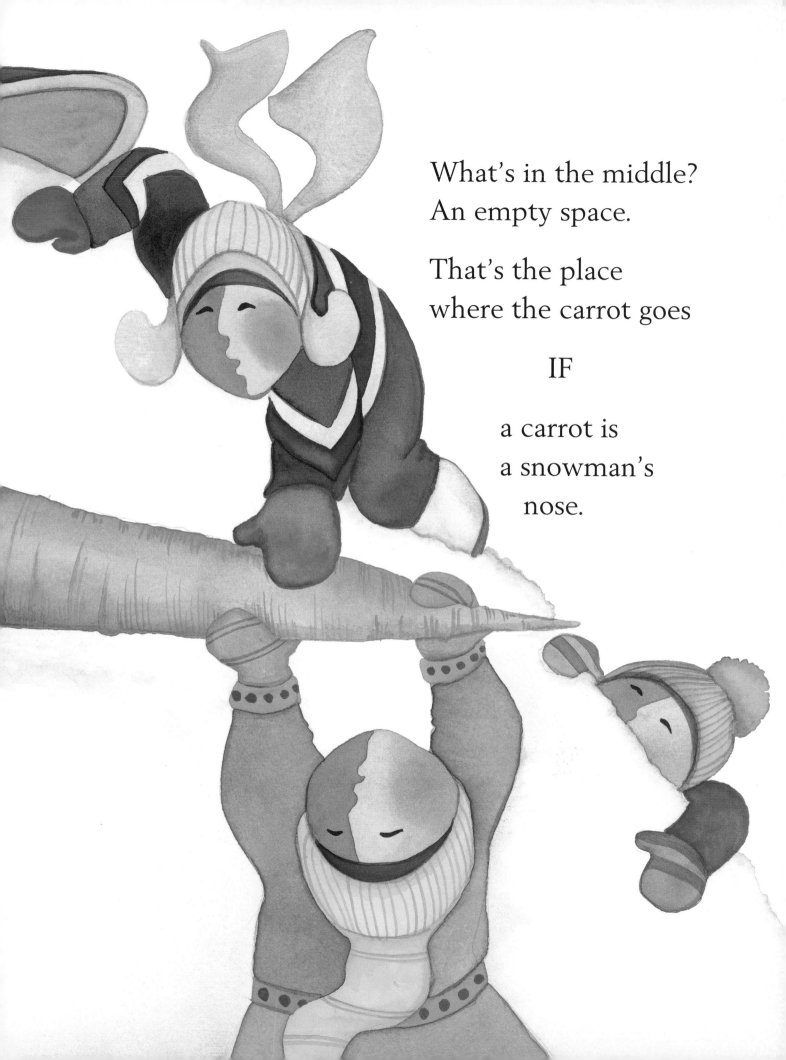

What's in the middle?
An empty space.

That's the place
where the carrot goes

IF

a carrot is
a snowman's
nose.

*But what about clothes?*

Walnut buttons,
five in a row,
belt in the middle,
boots below,
big wool scarf,
broom to hold,
mittens (in case his hands get cold),
earmuffs,
fanny pack,
something to read—

that's absolutely ALL you need

for a snowman.

Uh-oh....

Look in the sky again.
One small snowflake falling,

then...

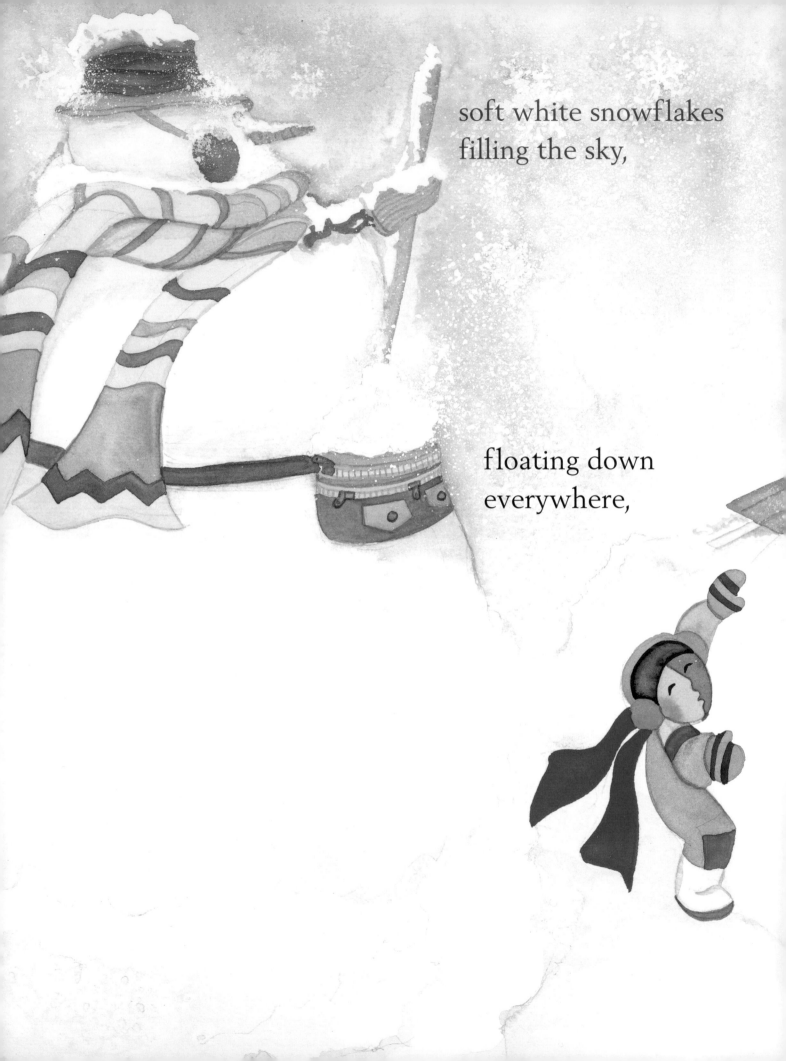

soft white snowflakes
filling the sky,

floating down
everywhere,

piling up high . . .

and THAT'S
all you need

for a snowman's
friend.

The end.